This book belongs to

....

....

EGMONT

We bring stories to life

First published in Great Britain in 2016 by Egmont UK Limited
The Yellow Building, 1 Nicholas Road, London W11 4AN

Written by Ronne Randall
Designed by Martin Aggett
Illustrated by Robin Davies
Endpaper illustrations by Dan Crisp

Thomas the Tank Engine & Friends ™

CREATED BY BRITT ALLCROFT

Based on the Railway Series by the Reverend W Awdry
© 2016 Gullane (Thomas) LLC. Thomas the Tank Engine & Friends and
Thomas & Friends are trademarks of Gullane (Thomas) Limited.
Thomas the Tank Engine & Friends and Design is Reg. U.S. Pat. & Tm. Off.
© 2016 HIT Entertainment Limited.

ISBN 978 1 4052 8126 3
62921/1

Printed in Italy

Stay safe online. Any website addresses listed in this book are correct
at the time of going to print. However, Egmont is not responsible for content
hosted by third parties. Please be aware that online content can be subject
to change and websites can contain content that is unsuitable for children.
We advise that all children are supervised when using the Internet.

FSC
MIX
Paper
FSC® C018306

Egmont is passionate about helping to preserve the world's remaining ancient forests.
We only use paper from legal and sustainable forest sources.

This book is made from paper certified by the Forest Stewardship Council® (FSC®),
an organisation dedicated to promoting responsible management of forest resources.
For more information on the FSC, please visit www.fsc.org. To learn more about Egmont's
sustainable paper policy, please visit www.egmont.co.uk/ethical

A Visit to London for
Thomas the Tank Engine

This is a story about how Thomas the Tank Engine helped The Fat Controller have a very special day in London!

Thomas the Tank Engine and Henry, Gordon and Edward were all shiny and polished. Their Drivers wanted them to look their best.

The Fat Controller was going to choose one of them to do a very special job!

The Fat Controller
inspected each engine.

Finally he announced, "Thomas, I choose you to take me and Lady Hatt to London to meet the **Queen!** We must get to Big Ben at four o'clock for the start of her birthday celebrations."

None of the engines were sure who Big Ben was but Thomas shivered with excitement. He would be meeting the Queen and going to London, the biggest city in the land!

The next morning, Thomas was coupled up to Annie, who carried The Fat Controller and Lady Hatt.

They chugged off to Brendam Docks, where Cranky was waiting to put them on the ferry to the Mainland.

"That ferry is late again!" said Cranky crossly. "You'll have to hurry if you want to arrive in London on time."

On the Mainland, Thomas puffed
through the countryside...

...and past a big train going the other way.
"Peep! Peep!" called Thomas.
"Wheeeeeeeee!" the train whistled back.

"Mustn't be late! Mustn't be late!"
Thomas puffed. "It's already two o'clock."

"Hurry! Hurry! Hurry!" he panted as, at last, roofs and chimneys came into sight.

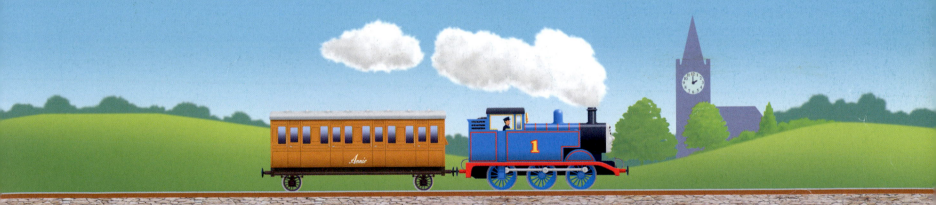

"Good work, Thomas!" said his Driver.
"We've arrived in Greenwich. That building is
the Royal Observatory. They have a telescope
there that can see all the way to the stars!"

"Can it see as far as Sodor?"
Thomas asked.

"Much further!" laughed his Driver.

At the River Thames, Thomas was told that they would be finishing the journey by boat.

Thomas saw a big sailing ship. "Is that the boat?" he wondered.

"No," said his Driver, smiling. "That is a very old ship called the *Cutty Sark*. It used to bring tea all the way from China."

Thomas had never heard about so many faraway places in just one day!

All at once there was a merry **TOOT! TOOT!**

"I'm Dilly," said a friendly barge. "I'll take you into London and show you some sights along the way!"

"It's three o'clock," Thomas said nervously. "We mustn't be late for the Queen and Big Ben!"

"I'll have you there quicker than you can say 'Piccadilly Circus!'" Dilly promised.

With Thomas and Annie safely aboard, Dilly set off. A big bridge loomed up in front of them. To Thomas' amazement, it opened up to let them through!

"This is Tower Bridge," Dilly told him. "And there is the Tower of London. It's almost a thousand years old!"

"The dome is St Paul's Cathedral," Dilly said. "It was built after the Great Fire of London, more than three hundred years ago."

"That's The Shard," said Dilly. "It's the tallest building in England!"

"That big wheel is the London Eye," Dilly went on. "From the top you can see all over London!"

"These are the Houses of Parliament," Dilly explained. "This is where laws are made. And there is the Elizabeth Tower, with its huge bell, Big Ben."

Suddenly there was a loud
BONG! BONG! BONG! BONG!

"Four o'clock!" said Dilly. "We're
right on time!"

"So that's Big Ben," laughed Thomas
looking up at the big clock.

As Dilly pulled up at Westminster, the Royal party came out onto the terrace.

The Queen thanked The Fat Controller for running such a fine Railway.

"I couldn't do it without Thomas and my other Really Useful Engines," replied The Fat Controller.

Thomas beamed from buffer to buffer.

That evening, as Thomas, Annie and Dilly rested on the Thames, brilliant fireworks lit up the sky.

CRACKLE! WHOOOOSHH! BOOM!

Thomas couldn't wait to tell his friends on Sodor about Big Ben, meeting the Queen and everything he'd seen in the biggest city in the land.

About the author

The Reverend W. Awdry was the creator of 26 little books about Thomas and his famous engine friends, the first being published in 1945. The stories came about when the Reverend's two-year-old son Christopher was ill in bed with the measles. Awdry invented stories to amuse him, which Christopher then asked to hear time and time again. And now for 70 years, children all around the world have been asking to hear these stories about Thomas, Edward, Gordon, James and the many other Really Useful Engines.

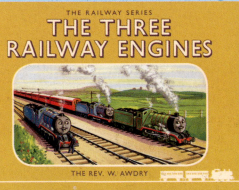

The Three Railway Engines, first published in 1945.

The Reverend Awdry with some of his readers at a model railway exhibition.